Who wants to be a poodle

I don't

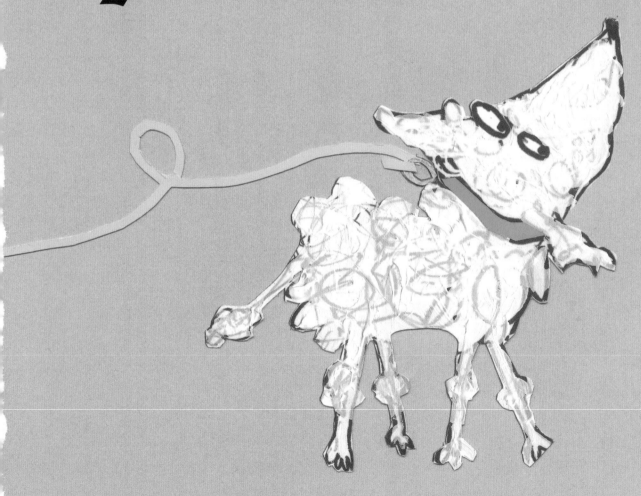

 **CANDLEWICK PRESS**

lauren child

A Cautionary Tale
for Verity,

who would love nothing better
than to dress her cat in a little bonnet

IN
a sumptuous apartment in a
fashionable city lived the elegantly rich and
divinely glamorous Mademoiselle Verity Brulée.

Verity Brulée did little with her time but shop for shoes
and visit the beauty parlor to have her wrinkles
smoothed and her eyelashes
lengthened.

She was the kind of person who liked everything to be "just so."

ALONG with Verity Brulée, with her very own personal bedroom, lived **Trixie Twinkle Toes Trot-a-Lot Delight**

    or **Trixie Toes** for short

    or **Trixie Twinkle Belle**

    or **Trixie Belle Baby,**

depending on Verity's mood.

The little poodle lived in the lap of luxury, with every creature comfort just a manicured paw away.

and a cook to prepare her n i b b l e s

There was a maid to plump her pillows

and a butler to carry her over the puddles.

And she was much adored
by Mademoiselle Brulée.

BUT Trixie Twinkle Toes was not happy.
For a start, she didn't like her name;
it was far too poodley.

She didn't like
the
puffing

or the
poofing

or
the
preening.

She didn't like the posing or the prancing.

She didn't like the perfuming the powdering or the pompoms.

And she didn't like the way Verity Brulée kept dressing her up in little pink ponchos.

THE thing was, Trixie Twinkle Toes just wasn't a poodle sort of person.
"No, I am just not cut out for a life of poodlery," she said to herself.
"I want to step in puddles."

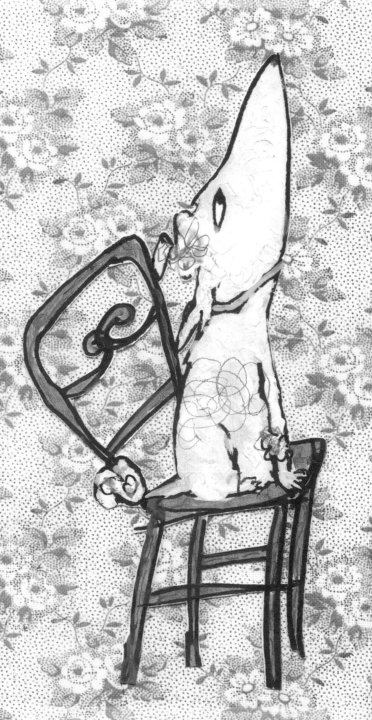

But of course she
kept these thoughts to herself.

Mademoiselle Verity Brulée never went out if the weather
was wet or indeed cloudy, stormy, snowy, or in fact
anything but fine. Her shoes were very expensive,
and she could not risk them being spoiled.

This meant
the two of them
were usually stuck
inside their
apartment—

Verity Brulée
idly flicking
through shoe
catalogs

while
Trixie Twinkle Toes
chewed on her pink
velvet ribbon.

And it was an uneventful life for the both of them.

ON fine days, the two of them would go out prancing in the park, though Verity never permitted the little poodle to stray from the path for fear of muddy paws. Trixie Twinkle Toes

"That's what a REAL dog should do," she would think, sighing a deep sigh.

chasing nothing in particular.

would peer over at the other dogs scampering about with sticks, paddling in puddles, and

Mademoiselle Brulée often mistook these sighs for little coughs and would wrap another little scarf around poor Trixie Twinkle Toes' neck.

ONE night Trixie Twinkle Toes was lying in her room,
listening to the real dogs howling at the moon.
As far as she could tell,
they were all called
names like

Growler
and
Gripper
and
Chomper
and
Squasher.

"That's what a dog's name should be," thought Trixie Twinkle Toes, looking into her full-length mirror. But what she saw just didn't look like someone who would ever be called Squasher. Pompommed toy poodles just aren't.

"I hate being a poooodle,"

she howled in a most un-poodle-like fashion.

WHICH woke Mademoiselle Brulée from her anxious dreams.

She popped on her kitten-heeled mules and click-clacked her way down the hall.

VERITY Brulée took a good look at
Trixie Twinkle Toes Trot-a-Lot Delight and said,
"Heavens, what is the matter with you,
my forlorn furry friend?"

And she rang for the maid,

who summoned the vet, who, after concocting

many tests and treatments, could find nothing wrong with the little dog.

Other than a slightly sore throat.

fleas flee

To cheer her up, the following day Verity Brulée took Trixie Twinkle Toes to the poodle parlor *Hound Heaven.*

While under the dryer, idly flicking through the latest issue of *Posh Pooch Monthly,*

Trixie Twinkle Toes noticed an article titled "How to Change Your Dog Image."

It showed a photograph of an unruly, scruffy-looking dog and next to it a picture of the same dog all neat and tidy and the words *three months later.*

"Of course," she thought, "if a dog can be cleaned and preened, then it can also be scruffed and roughed."

"I will change my image," she said as she sipped her cappoochino.

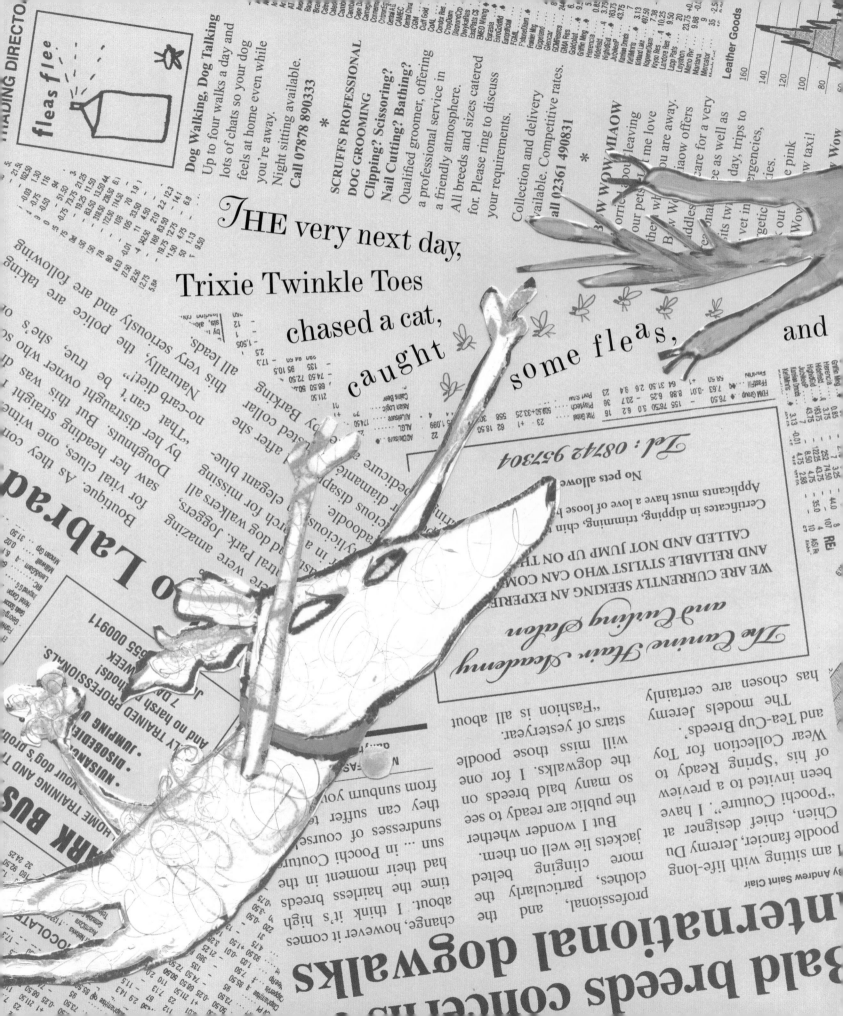

THE very next day,

Trixie Twinkle Toes

chased a cat,

caught

some fleas,

and

chewed Mr. Chomley's newspaper.

Verity Brulée, utterly alarmed, telephoned her pet psychic to see if she could find out just what strange force was troubling her little dog.

MR. Agunadi looked
into Mademoiselle
Verity
Brulée's
teacup
but could see
nothing
but

two
lonely
tea leaves.

Then he looked at

"Oh, good grief, I have caught fleas! I foresee a trip to the pet parlor."

I feel itchy.

I sense a thousand tiny teeth.

I am getting a weird sensation.

"I," said and paw Trixie Twinkle Toes'

VERITY Brulée had
Trixie Twinkle Toes
kept indoors,
de-flea-ed,

and given another
helping of the finest
dishy dog food.

Trixie Twinkle Toes felt relieved.
She found cats boring, fleas itchy, and newspapers rather bland.

ONE rainy day later,
Trixie Twinkle Toes was
idly watching TV when up popped
a commercial for

**THE GREATEST
DOG ACT
ON EARTH.**

The voice said,

**"BE ASTOUNDED,
BE AMAZED,
BE BAMBOOZLED
BY THE PERFORMING
POODLE SISTERS!"**
And then she
saw the words

**DAZZLINGLY
DANGEROUS
DARING DOGS!**

Trixie Twinkle Toes had never even heard of
a poodle being DANGEROUS or DARING
but she liked the idea of it.

"I will become **DANGEROUS** and **DARING**," she said, hopping off her pile of feather pillows.

But who would believe such a thing, even if they had been listening.

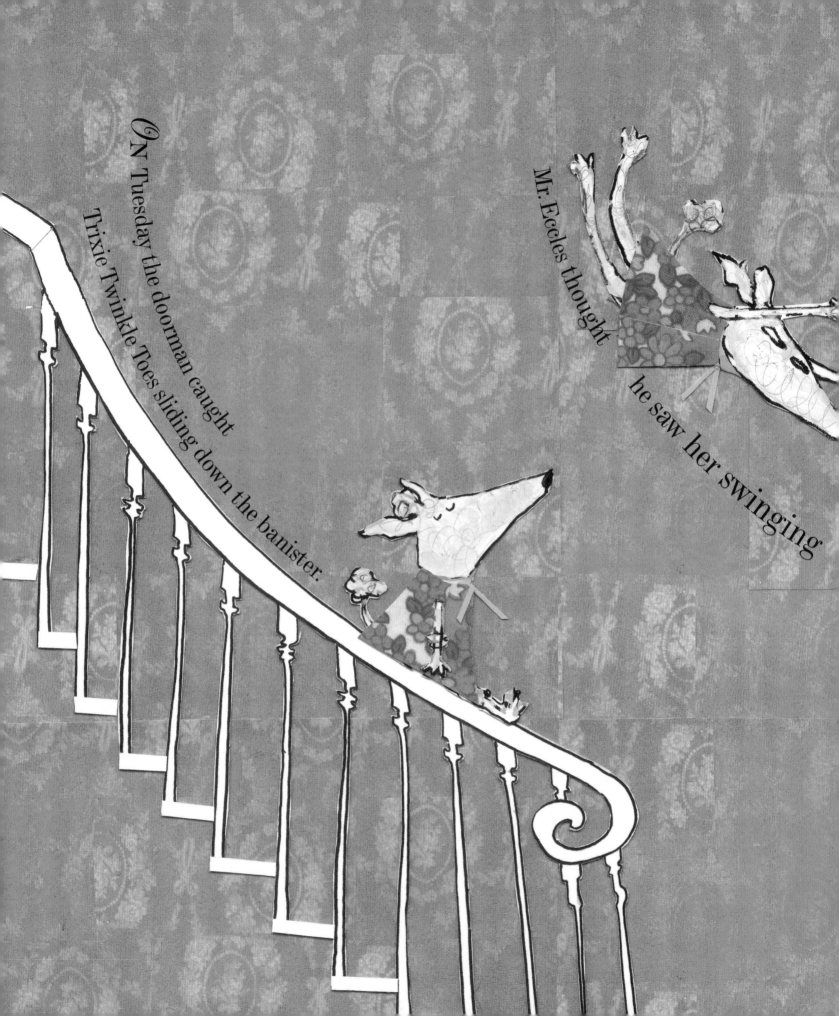

ON Tuesday the doorman caught
Trixie Twinkle Toes sliding down the banister.

Mr. Eccles thought
he saw her swinging

on the chandelier,

and Mrs. Grover, the dog walker,

Trixie Twinkle Toes swore she spotted diving into the ornamental fountain.

VERITY Brulée, shocked by this astonishing behavior, rang down to the doorman, who ordered a car to drive Trixie Twinkle Toes Trot-a-Lot Delight to the pooch psychiatrist on the double!

"Qu

iCk! Step on it!"

THE psychiatrist got
Trixie Twinkle Toes
to do some very
tricky tests.

He even tried
hypnosis, but he just
could not discover
what was wrong.

At last, exasperated, he sighed, "What is the trouble, my small canine client?"

"I want to stick my head out of car windows and feel the wind in my ears. I want to bark at dogs in the street. I want to catch sticks and roll in the mud. I want to be DANGEROUS and DARING, but most of all, I want to step in puddles."

But of course the psychiatrist could not understand her.

BY the time Verity Brulée and Trixie Twinkle Toes stepped out of the psychiatrist's office, rain was pouring down and beautiful pools of water were forming everywhere.

Trixie

looked

longingly

at the

deep

gray

puddles

but

said

nothing.

Until suddenly Trixie Twinkle Toes heard a terrible sound. It was the howl of a tiny drowning hound.

In one DAZZLING moment, she slid down the railing, took a DARING leap into the air, and DANGEROUSLY dove into the deepest puddle, instantly ruining her shoes. Verity Brulée, fearing her little dog was in great danger, waded in after her.

BUT to Verity's astonishment, there was Trixie Twinkle Toes, not drowning but holding up the bedraggled Chihuahua.

"What a DOG!" exclaimed the owner. "You have saved little Gripper from certain death!"

Verity Brulée looked at Trixie Twinkle Toes and saw not a little pompommed toy poodle but instead a

DAZZLINGLY
DANGEROUS
DARING
dog.

Trixie Twinkle Toes barked, and suddenly Verity Brulée understood every word.

FROM that day on, Mademoiselle Verity Brulée and Trixie Twinkle Toes eagerly read the weather pages—and if it was raining, they went out with all the other dogs.

And Verity never made Trixie Twinkle Toes wear a hat, a scarf, or even a poncho ever again.

Though however much Trixie Twinkle Toes tried, she just could not get Verity to understand one important thing....

"Trixie Twinkle Toes Trot-a-Lot Delight!"

DAZZLINGLY
DANGEROUS
DARING dogs
do not like to be called silly names.